W9-DGB-470

KEKE PALMER

Joanne Mattern

Mitchell Lane
PUBLISHERS

P.O. Box 196
Hockessin, Delaware 19707
Visit us on the web: www.mitchelllane.com
Comments? email us: mitchelllane@mitchelllane.com

Mitchell Lane
PUBLISHERS

Printing   1   2   3   4   5   6   7   8   9

A Robbie Reader
Contemporary Biography

Abigail Breslin	Albert Pujols	Alex Rodriguez
Aly and AJ	Amanda Bynes	AnnaSophia Robb
Ashley Tisdale	Brenda Song	Brittany Murphy
Charles Schulz	Dakota Fanning	Dale Earnhardt Jr.
David Archuleta	Demi Lovato	Donovan McNabb
Drake Bell & Josh Peck	Dr. Seuss	Dwayne "The Rock" Johnson
Dylan & Cole Sprouse	Eli Manning	Emily Osment
Emma Watson	Hilary Duff	Jaden Smith
Jamie Lynn Spears	Jennette McCurdy	Jesse McCartney
Jimmie Johnson	Johnny Gruelle	Jonas Brothers
Jordin Sparks	Justin Bieber	Keke Palmer
Larry Fitzgerald	LeBron James	Mia Hamm
Miley Cyrus	Miranda Cosgrove	Raven-Symoné
Selena Gomez	Shaquille O'Neal	Story of Harley-Davidson
Syd Hoff	Taylor Lautner	Tiki Barber
Tom Brady	Tony Hawk	Victoria Justice
Tony Hawk		

Library of Congress Cataloging-in-Publication Data
Mattern, Joanne, 1963–
  Keke Palmer / by Joanne Mattern.
     p. cm. — (A Robbie reader)
  Includes bibliographical references and index.
  Includes webliography.
  ISBN 978-1-58415-896-7 (library bound)
  1. Palmer, Keke—Juvenile literature. 2. Motion picture actors and actresses—United States
Biography—Juvenile literature. 3. Singers—United States—Biography—Juvenile literature.
I. Title.
PN2287.P2245M38 2010
791.430'28092—dc22
[B]
                                                                        2010019388

ABOUT THE AUTHOR: Joanne Mattern is the author of more than 300 books for children. She has written biographies about many famous people for Mitchell Lane Publishers, including the Jonas Brothers, Jaden Smith, Michelle Obama, Peyton Manning, and Albert Pujols. Joanne also enjoys writing about animals, reading, and being outdoors. She lives in New York State with her husband, four children, and several pets.

PUBLISHER'S NOTE: The following story has been thoroughly researched and to the best of our knowledge represents a true story. While every possible effort has been made to ensure accuracy, the publisher will not assume liability for damages caused by inaccuracies in the data, and makes no warranty on the accuracy of the information contained herein. This story has not been authorized or endorsed by Keke Palmer.

TABLE OF CONTENTS

Words in **bold** type can be found in the glossary.

Keke Palmer started her acting and music careers early. On July 25, 2009, she appeared on *The Tonight Show with Conan O'Brien*. Keke talked about her movie and TV projects, and she shared her everyday concerns about turning sixteen, dating, and learning how to drive.

Born to Be a Star

Little Keke Palmer had been begging her mother for weeks. She wanted to sing with the **choir** (KWY-ur) in the church that the family attended. Mrs. Palmer was firm. Keke was only five years old. She was not old enough to perform with the church choir. She would have to wait until she was at least ten.

Keke was young, but she was also determined. She kept asking her mother to let her sing. Her family knew Keke had a great voice. Finally, Mrs. Palmer and the choir director agreed.

Little Keke was very excited the first time she sat with the choir. When it came time to sing, she stood up next to her mother. The

Keke started singing in her church choir, and the training she received there paid off. Keke often performs in public, including at a charity concert in 2008.

director gave the signal to begin. The first hymn was "Jesus Loves Me." Keke opened her mouth and began to sing. She sang as loud as she could.

Keke sang so loud that no one could hear the other choir members. Her mother stopped singing. So did the rest of the choir. Five-year-old Keke was singing solo!

The choir director could not believe what a strong, beautiful voice Keke had. He made her a full member of the church choir. It would not be long before people all over the United States would learn about Keke and her talents. The little girl who sang with her church choir would grow up to be one of the busiest young actresses in Hollywood.

Keke shares a tender moment with her father. Both of Keke's parents come from large families, and the Palmers share strong family values.

A Happy Family

Keke Palmer's parents, Sharon and Lawrence, met when they were in college. They quickly fell in love and got married after they finished school. Soon afterward, they moved to Chicago. They both found jobs with the Black **Ensemble** (on-SOM-bul) Theater. This theater group was famous in Chicago.

Family was very important to the Palmers. In 1991, their first child was born. They named their new daughter L'Oreal (lor-ee-AL). The Palmers had their second daughter on August 26, 1993. They named her Lauren Keyana Palmer.

L'Oreal was happy to have a little sister, but she did not like the baby's name. She

9

had an **imaginary** (ih-MAJ-un-nayr-ee) friend named Keke. She wanted her parents to name the baby Keke after her friend. Sharon and Lawrence said no, but L'Oreal called the baby Keke anyway! Soon, many other people called Lauren Keke as well.

Keke was a happy child with a big **personality** (pur-suh-NAL-uh-tee). She was always talking and showing off. She and L'Oreal spent a lot of time backstage at the Black Ensemble Theater. Keke watched the actors rehearse and saw firsthand how shows are created. She later said that she got a lot of her acting skills just from watching those performances. She told *Black Star News*, "I did not want to take acting lessons because I don't think anyone can teach you how to act. You have to find that in yourself."

When L'Oreal and Keke were young, Sharon got a job as a teacher. Lawrence worked as a salesman for a company that made plastic products. In 2001, the family grew bigger when Sharon gave birth to twins. They

Keke snuggles with her younger sister and brother, who are twins. Twins run in the Palmer family—both her mother and father are part of sets of twins!

named the little boy Lawrence and the little girl Lawrencia after their father.

The Palmers spent a lot of time singing and performing at their home in Robbins, Illinois. They were also active in their church. Even though Mr. and Mrs. Palmer no longer acted onstage, Keke was interested in performing. Her parents encouraged her to follow her dreams. Soon she would have her first chance to be onstage.

As Keke kept acting and enjoying her work, her fame grew.

Keke's Big Move

Keke acted in school plays and sang in school concerts. Then, when she was nine years old, her mother saw an ad in the newspaper. A theater company in Chicago was holding **auditions** (aw-DIH-shuns) for *The Lion King*. Keke couldn't wait to try out. "I love to sing. I love to dance. So maybe I'd try to act," she said.

Keke and her father traveled to Chicago. More than 1,000 children were at the audition. The show's **casting director** liked Keke a lot. He asked her to come back and audition again. Keke made it through several auditions. When there were only fifteen children left, Keke got some bad news. The casting director did not choose her to go on.

Keke first worked with Ice Cube in *Barbershop 2.* She was thrilled to work with him again in *The Longshots.* She said, "It was definitely cool to get to know him better. He's so cool, laid back—definitely a family guy."

Keke did not get discouraged. She later said, "I did pretty good for my first time auditioning so I decided that it was fun and I wanted to keep on doing it." Her parents decided that she needed an agent. An agent would help her find acting jobs.

Keke's new agent soon found her a great job. In 2003, she won a small part in the movie *Barbershop 2: Back in Business*. It was filming in Chicago. Keke got to work with famous actors like Queen Latifah, Cedric the Entertainer, and Ice Cube. She had a great time making the movie. She also enjoyed seeing strong African-American role models. Her parents had always told her she could do anything she wanted to, and working on *Barbershop 2* showed her that this was true.

Keke couldn't wait to find more acting jobs after she finished making *Barbershop 2*. There was just one problem. Most movies and television shows are filmed in Hollywood. To get really good jobs, Keke and her family would have to move to California.

At first, the Palmers did not want to move. Then, in November 2003, Mr. Palmer was offered a good job in a town near Hollywood. The family talked and prayed about what they should do. They realized that moving to Hollywood would give Keke the best chance to make her dreams come true. They left their home and started their new life in California.

Keke's rise to the big screen was fast. By the time she was thirteen, she was working with Tyler Perry, a big director in Hollywood.

Keke in the Movies

Keke did not waste any time finding acting jobs. She appeared in several television commercials. She also was a guest star in a few television shows, including *Strong Medicine* and *Cold Case*.

Keke also starred in a television movie called *The Wool Cap*. This movie tells the story of a lonely building manager who cannot speak. He has to take care of a talkative young girl. Keke was happy to play the girl. She was even more excited when she found out that actor William H. Macy starred in the movie. Macy was Keke's favorite actor. At first, meeting him was scary for the young fan. "I went in to the audition and got so scared because William H. Macy was in the room," she told the television

Working with William H. Macy in *The Wool Cap* was a dream come true for Keke, who had been a fan of the actor for a long time. She said that during the film, Macy "was just such a helpful actor and I really looked up to him after that. He was so nice to me and he gave me time. I really respect him for that."

network TNT. Even though she was nervous, she took a deep breath and read her lines. Although she wouldn't hear from the directors for a while, she kept practicing her lines. Good thing she did, because she got the part!

Critics (KRIH-tiks) thought she was wonderful. Keke was even **nominated** (NAH-mih-nay-ted) for a Screen Actors Guild Award for her performance. She was eleven years old and the youngest person ever nominated for a leading role. Even though she did not win, Keke and her family knew it was a great honor to receive the nomination.

Keke was about to go on to even more success. In 2005, she auditioned for a movie called *Akeelah and the Bee*. This movie is about a girl from a poor neighborhood who competes in the Scripps National Spelling Bee. When Keke got the part, she knew she would have to work hard. The character she plays is tough, but she is also scared and hurt.

Doug Atchison, the film's director, knew Keke was perfect for the part as soon as he saw her. "It was powerful the way she read," he said in *The Making of Akeelah and the Bee*. "So I knew she was special then."

Akeelah and the Bee was released in 2006. Critics were delighted with Keke's performance. Once again, she was nominated for many different awards.

Although Keke lives in California, she often travels to New York City. In 2009, she appeared in the Macy's Thanksgiving Day Parade, and in 2010 she joined the excitement of New York's annual Fashion Week.

Keke is one of Nickelodeon's brightest stars. In 2010, she joined fellow Nick star Miranda Cosgrove to present First Lady Michelle Obama with a Big Help Award.

In 2006, Keke also worked with famous director Tyler Perry for the first time. She was cast in his movie *Madea's Family Reunion*. Keke played a tough foster child named Nikki Grady. She would go on to play Nikki again in Perry's 2009 movie *Madea Goes to Jail*, as well as on an **episode** (EH-pih-sohd) of Perry's television show *Tyler Perry's House of Payne*.

Keke was now a star. However, her next role would take her in a completely different direction.

Keke and Corbin Bleu costarred in *Jump In!* She told the press, "Oh, Corbin! I had a lot of fun with him. Working with him was awesome."

TV, Music, and More

Keke went on to make several more television movies. She starred with Corbin Bleu in the popular Disney movie *Jump In!*, the drama *Cleaner*, and a true story about a female football player called *The Longshots*. Keke enjoyed making these movies, but she realized that most of the characters she played weren't like her. She was a silly person. Keke wanted to show people how funny she was. Finally, she got her chance.

In 2008, Keke won the title role for a Nickelodeon television series called *True Jackson, VP*. The show is about a teenager, True Jackson, who gets her own fashion line at a design company. True realizes that even though she is working with adults, the design company is a lot like high school. She has to deal with friendship troubles, romance, **cliques** (KLEEKS or KLIKS), and jealousy. The show is humorous but touches on real issues that all teens face.

Keke has enjoyed playing True. She loves making people laugh. "I've always been a comedian in my family," she told *Blogcritics*. "It was kind of weird that I've always been the serious role. Playing comedy is a lot easier–not necessarily easier, but more natural–because it's always been what I have done."

In 2009, Keke had one more thing in common with True Jackson. She designed her own clothing line for Walmart. The low-priced fashions include dresses, shirts, leggings, and more, all aimed at young teens.

True Jackson, VP, also allowed Keke to express herself through music. She wrote and sang the show's theme song. Keke had never given up on her music. In 2007, she had released her first music CD, *So Uncool*. The songs on the album were upbeat and **appropriate** (uh-PROH-pree-ut) for young

In 2010, Keke won an NAACP Image Award. This award honors African Americans who create positive and uplifting images in the media and serve as role models for the community.

teens. Keke and her family hoped the album would be a big success.

Keke's record company had a different plan for her. Atlantic Records wanted her to perform songs that Keke thought were not appropriate for young girls. They also wanted her to wear clothes that were not suitable for teenagers. Keke did not feel comfortable with this type of image. She refused to do what Atlantic Records wanted. For that reason, Atlantic did not promote the album. Keke was hurt, but she was proud that she had stood by her principles. In 2009, she signed with Interscope Records and began working on her second album.

Even though she is busy with her television show and other work, Keke makes time to help others. She is active in several **charities** (CHAYR-uh-teez) that help children. One of her favorite charities is the Boys and Girls Clubs of America. Boys and Girls Clubs provide role models and positive activities for children. Keke often speaks to groups of teenagers for a program called It's Cool to Be Smart. "I love trying to motivate [MOH-tih-vayt] and inspire them and let them know there is more out there in life than the neighborhood they live in," she told *Daily Variety.*

Keke also spends a lot of time with her family. She says that her family is the real secret behind her success. She told the *Amsterdam News,* "My family is proud of me

Keke enjoys performing at charity events such as the Variety Power of Youth event. This event focuses on getting young people to work for charity.

and I am proud of myself." They all have reason to be very proud of Keke's attitude and her success.

CHRONOLOGY

1993 Lauren Keyana "Keke" Palmer is born on August 26.

2002 Keke auditions for a role in a touring production of *The Lion King*.

2003 Keke is cast in her first movie, *Barbershop 2: Back in Business*; the Palmers move to Hollywood.

2004 Keke stars in the television movie *The Wool Cap*.

2006 Keke stars in *Akeelah and the Bee*; she appears in *Madea's Family Reunion*.

2007 Keke stars in the Disney movie *Jump In!* and has a role in the movie *Cleaner*; she releases her first CD, *So Uncool*.

2008 Keke stars in the movie *The Longshots*; she stars in the Nick television series *True Jackson, VP*.

2009 Keke appears in the movie *Madea Goes to Jail*; she designs a line of clothes for Walmart.

2010 Keke Palmer wins an NAACP Image Award; she releases her second CD, titled *Keke Palmer*.

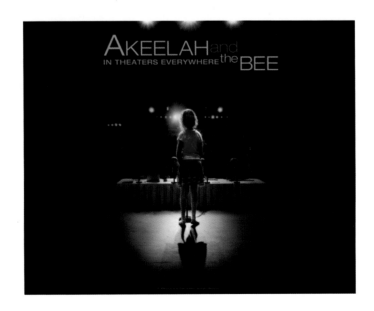

FILMOGRAPHY

Movies

2009	*Madea Goes to Jail*
2008	*The Longshots*
2007	*Jump In!* (TV)
	Cleaner
2006	*Akeelah and the Bee*
	Madea's Family Reunion
2005	*Knights of the South Bronx* (TV)
2004	*Barbershop 2: Back in Business*
	The Wool Cap (TV)

TV Shows

2010	*7 Secrets: Keke Palmer*
2008–present	*True Jackson, VP*
2007	*Just Jackson*
	Tyler Perry's House of Payne
2005	*Law & Order: Special Victims Unit*
	ER
	Second Time Around
2004	*Cold Case*
	Strong Medicine

DISCOGRAPHY

2010	*Keke Palmer*
2007	*So Uncool*

FIND OUT MORE

Books

If you enjoyed this book about Keke Palmer, you might also enjoy the following Robbie Reader Contemporary Biographies from Mitchell Lane Publishers:

Demi Lovato

Jennette McCurdy

Miranda Cosgrove

Raven-Symoné

Selena Gomez

Victoria Justice

Works Consulted

"BEE-ing Keke." *Weekly Reader News*—Senior, April 28, 2006, Vol. 84, Issue 24.

Forr, Amanda. "Keke Palmer: The New VP." *Girls' Life*, December 2008/January 2009, Vol. 15, Issue 3.

Henderson, Shirley. "5 Questions for Keke Palmer." *Ebony*, December 2007, Vol. 63, Issue 2.

———. "Turning the Keys to Success." *Ebony*, March 2010, Vol. 65, Issue 5.

Lewis-Boothman, Debra. "Nick's New Teen Star." *People*, January 19, 2009, Vol. 71, Issue 2.

McNamara, Tara. "Keke Palmer: Helping Motivate and Inspire Through the Boys & Girls Clubs of America." *Daily Variety*, December 4, 2009, Vol. 305, Issue 43.

"Movies on TNT: *The Wool Cap.*" http://www.tnt.tv/movies/movietitle/?oid=5975

Odesanya, Olayemi. "Keke Palmer at Macy's Parade." *New York Amsterdam News*, November 26, 2009, Vol. 100, Issue 48.

"Profile: Keke Palmer." http://blackstarnews.com/news/135/ARTICLE/2077/2006-04-27.html

Pumilia, Maddy. "A Chat With Keke Palmer, Star of Nickelodeon's *True Jackson, VP.*" *Blogcritics*, October 19, 2008. http://blogcritics.org/video/article/a-chat-with-keke-palmer-star/

On the Internet

Internet Movie Database: Keke Palmer
    http://www.imdb.com/name/nm/1551130

Keke Palmer #1 Fan Site
    http://www.keke-palmer.org

Official Keke Palmer Web Site
    http://www.kekepalmer.com

True Jackson, VP Web Site
    http://www.nick.com/shows/trujacksonvp

GLOSSARY

appropriate (uh-PROH-pree-ut)—Suitable or right.

audition (aw-DIH-shun)—A tryout for a part in a play, concert, or movie.

casting director (KAS-ting duh-REK-tur)—The person responsible for giving actors jobs in movies, TV shows, or plays.

charities (CHAYR-uh-teez)—Groups that raise money to help people in need.

choir (KWY-ur)—A group of people that sings together, often in a church.

clique (KLEEK, or KLIK)—A small group of people who do not accept other people into their group.

critics (KRIH-tiks)—People who review movies, plays, TV shows, or books.

ensemble (on-SOM-bul)—A group of musicians or actors who perform together.

episode (EH-pih-sohd)—A program in a TV series.

imaginary (ih-MAJ-uh-nayr-ee)—Make-believe; not real.

nominated (NAH-mih-nay-tid)—Named as a possibility for receiving an award.

personality (pur-suh-NAL-uh-tee)—The qualities that make a person act the way he or she does.

INDEX